WRITTEN

Written
Poetry and Prose by Inmates of His Majesty's Prisons
St. Vincent and the Grenadines

Published by Hobo Jungle Press
St. Vincent & the Grenadines, W.I.
Sharon, Connecticut, USA

ISBN #979-8-9897406-7-3
Library of Congress Control Number: 2024950100
First edition
January 2025

Illustrations by Alana Hudson

WRITTEN

Poetry and Prose
by Inmates of His Majesty's Prisons
St. Vincent and the Grenadines

Compiled by David "Darkie" Williams
Edited by Hobo Jungle Press

Contents

Foreword

I have always publicly expressed the fact that St. Vincent and the Grenadines is a huge reservoir of natural talent, and that all it needs is for someone to take an interest in it, deep enough to try to harness it and expose it to the rest of the world.

Across the Caribbean, writers of poetry and other literary forms are emerging every day. In St. Vincent and the Grenadines, seeds that had been planted by the likes of Tim Daisy, Ellsworth "Shake" Keane, Owen Campbell (who is regularly quoted by St. Vincent and the Grenadines Prime Minister Dr. Ralph Gonsalves), Cecil "Blazer" Williams, and the New Artist Movement (NAM), to name a few, have taken root and are now "throwing up innocent little daisies" from every corner of the country.

At this point in our history, there are over one hundred books of poetry authored by Vincentians. This collection comes to you from what I consider a most unusual and remote place: behind our prison walls.

All contributors to this volume are, or were, inmates of His Majesty's Prison and the Belle Isle Correctional Facility in St. Vincent, a place where, as Tim Daisy wrote: "The damp and brutal cold and moldy cell walls connive... and wheezing chests steer panic into the unsuspecting clutches that forms part of society's rif raf (sic). The great forgotten. The condemned."

Apparently, inmates were writing verses and other things that they were sharing with one another; as fate would have it, the authorities provided an opportunity for them to get some formalized, short-term, in house training that worked wonders in helping the inmates to understand the process better.

Although there were already pieces that contained con-
flict, created imagery and spectacle, this training (approx-
imately three months) gave them the ability to produce
more knowledge-based and theoretical works.

The genres were many: drama, love, rebellion, disap-
pointment, loss. The sky seemed to be the limit.

In St. Vincent, we have grown accustomed to the annual
Christmas concert put on by the inmates. In recent times,
an exhibition of hand-crafted items has been gaining
ascendency within the public domain. The abundance of
natural, creative abilities that resides behind those "walls"
are barely being touched, and this collection will further
emphasize that.

- David "Darkie" Williams

Prologue

It Was Written

They said, "Speak it into existence." So here it is.
A masterpiece.

In a place where people are alone with their five senses (in some cases there are six), a mysterious thing occurs. When loneliness and these senses mix, they produce thoughts that generate feelings, and through inspiration these feelings are expressed. Groomed and guided, these expressions morph into words that take the shape of stories and poetry, so they can be heard by you, the reader.

We had things on our chests we wanted to get off.
So pen to paper we took
To relieve stress and for internal peace.
We came up with this book.

It wasn't competitive;
We worked together,
But each at our own pace.
Inspired differently,
And using different recipes,
We cooked according to our own taste.

We served up love, hate, life, death, and a bit of humor,
Some sarcasm, some stoicism, some sensual, some social,
  and even some horror.

Our pieces will make you scream, shout, laugh, cry,
And tune in to your heart.
Some are factual, others fictional,
But each one, a work of art.

Who said big boys and girls don't cry? Really?

Read *Fwen*, *Inner Turmoil*, *My Time*, *Crossroads*, *Mark Me*, and *Farewell My Love*. We uncovered a lot, yet there's still much left covered from view.

What you didn't get in this edition, no worries. Look for it in volume two.

What more can we say? Thank you for reading. Thank you for allowing us to express ourselves and giving us something to believe in. Thank you, Darkie, for imparting your wisdom, Miss Dougan, Mrs. Edwards for encouraging expressive freedom. You saw the vision, admired the potential, and saw it to the end.

And because of that, behold, it was *WRITTEN*, and will be written again!

- Junior Jarvis

Junior Jarvis

Junior is an avid reader and writer. Born and raised in the heart of Kingstown, he spent more than half of his life informing the masses. Junior promises that there is much, much more to come in the form of poetry, short stories, novels, and plays.

The Promise

A crowd larger than the usual bathers had gathered on the small beach that overcast Sunday evening, mainly because of the spectacle being created by Calvin and Loretta as they haggled the way a man and his wayward wife would: Calvin trying his best to get her to leave the area without too much physical interaction, Loretta resisting — without being aggressive — so as not to attract unwanted attention.

They were not man and wife. Loretta was the lover — if you could still call her that — of Calvin's younger brother Adam, who had sailed away from that very beach exactly one year ago, promising to return one year later.

Loretta was in her Sunday best, waiting for Adam's return.

"Loretta, please, you have to believe me. Adam's not coming back. You have to believe me," Calvin said, maybe for the 10th or 15th time, each time more desperate than the last.

"He said he's coming back today and I'm waiting. Ada won't disappoint me."

Ada was Loretta's pet name for Adam, who called her Lynn out of his admiration for her and in homage to his favorite Country and Western singer, Loretta Lynn.

"You haven't heard from him for a whole year. Isn't that disappointing enough?"

"There must be a reason."

"There is."

"What? Tell me. What do you know for you to say that Ada's not coming? Did you hear from him? What do you know Calvin?"

"No. I didn't hear from him. Nobody's heard. But I know he's not coming back. Not today, Not anytime. He's not coming back. He's..." An exasperated Calvin stopped short.

The crowd on the beach got larger.

One Year Earlier

The morning was particularly chilly; cold enough for Adam Jeffery to put on one of his father's old British Army jackets. He estimated it would take about 12 hours to make it to Trinidad.

He knew, too, that at some point he would have to remove the jacket, but for now he needed the warmth.

He stood on the beach with Loretta, the love of his life, close behind her, arms over her shoulders, chin on the crown of her head. They were staring at the open ocean as the sun prepared to make its appearance. The sky was still dark, but clear and cloudless. The air was crisp. The beach was practically deserted, except for a few fishermen lazily making their way to their crafts. The gulls overhead cawed, looking for an early breakfast.

"You think we can do this?"

"We have to. We can't turn back now."

"I know. I know. I know. We got this."

"I love you."

"I love you too, babe."

Everybody loved Loretta McIntosh. Everybody. And while she appreciated and was humbled by the adoration from people in the Long Wall community and beyond, the 19-year-old only returned affection to Adam. Her first man. And if it were up to the two of them, her only man.

Loretta was a beautiful singer, but she wanted to be a teacher. Her calm, tender ways and soothing voice that went along with all the other attributes made her a suitable candidate for anything she decided to do.

Loretta adored Adam and he, her. They were childhood sweethearts ever since they were students at the Kingstown Anglican School. He was two years older. She admired him for his ambition and adventurous ways. She loved him because he supported her dreams and their plans to spend the rest of their lives together. And that's what brought them here on the beach today.

One night, four months ago on this very beach, but further down on the reclamation site where lovers hang out, Loretta once again shared her desire to teach. She was going to complete her home skills training program, then begin her school teacher's program. Within one year she would be qualified to teach young students.

Adam was excited and happy for her.

"You will be the best teacher ever. I wish I could be one of your little students," he had teased her.

"You will be my big student," she replied, playfully, as they lay on a large boulder looking up into the starry night sky.

"And thank you for supporting my plans," he said. "You know my dreams have you in them and they will come true, right?"

"I know that so far it's been good and it can only get better," she replied. "With me going to teaching school and you going to Trinidad for the time, that will set us up for a promising future."

About a year earlier, Adam had spoken to Loretta about a job opportunity he was told about by a friend. The idea was to travel to the twin island Republic of Trinidad and Tobago and secure a job at one of the many openings in the economically booming island. The friend had already traveled down "south" and had written to Adam, telling him a job was waiting for him on the friend's uncle's trawler, should he decide to venture. Loretta thought that as long as Adam felt strongly about the opportunity and believed it had the potential for growth, he should go for it.

Although Adam pulled his weight at home and was loyal to his father and brother (his mother had died from cancer years before), he didn't want to be tied down to the family's grocery store business. Not wanting to walk in his father's footsteps and wanting to get out of his older brother Cally's shadow, Adam bought a pirogue, which he used as a ferry/taxi service along the Kingstown shoreline during the busy days. When things were slow, he tried his hand at fishing. The sea was teeming with fishes from the Harbour Club, close to their home at Marshall yard, all the way to Rose Place, even around to Edinboro.

Adam was proud of his investment. He named the boat "Loretta Lynn" in homage to his love and his favorite Country and Western singer.

What made this plan so ambitious is that Adam intended to sail Loretta Lynn to Trinidad. The idea, which was deemed practicable by his friend and accepted by Loretta, was that when not trawling, they could ply a route on the sea around the base.

Now, on this chilly morning, Adam was ready to sail. He had packed Loretta Lynn with all he thought he needed for the trip: clothing, food and toiletries estimated to last his first two weeks in Trinidad, a first aid kit, extra fuel, a flare gun and flares, water, a machete sharpened on both sides, and a heavy duty pearl-handled utility knife that once belonged to his father.

Standing on the shore, they hardly spoke. They just held each other. She grasped his hands that were folded across her chest, resting gently on her breasts.

"You know I'm coming back right?"

 You promise?"

"Yes, I promise. A promise I will never break."

"I know."

"You waiting for me?"

"Yes, I will"

"You promise?"

"I promise."

"I know."

Behind them, someone cleared their throat, then spoke.

"Sorry to interrupt the farewell party."

They turned around. It was Calvin.

"You're late," Adam said, as he and Loretta approached Calvin. They had a short group hug.

"Little brother sailing off, leaving his fair maiden behind," Calvin said as they separated. "The bravest man in the world," he added.

"And the safest one too." Loretta said as she playfully punched him on his arm.

"I know," he said. "Anyway, it came over the radio weather report that they're expecting showers and rough seas by mid-morning. So, either you head out now, or postpone the sail of the "Titanic".

They laughed.

"Oh shucks!" Calvin snapped his fingers. "I was supposed to bring daddy's old rain cloak for you, but I forgot it at the shop front. Loretta, could you do me the favour and run for it please? I could give my farewell lecture and hug to my brother in the meantime."

"OK. Sure. I'll be right back," she said as she pecked Adam on the cheek and took the short jog to the store.

On her return, Loretta heard the familiar sound of Loretta Lynn's motor, seeming to be heading away from the beach. When the beach came into view, what she had believed and feared was true. Adam had set out without waiting for her. Without saying goodbye.

"Ada! Ada!" she shouted as she ran to the beach.

She stopped when she reached alongside Calvin. His pants and half his shirt were wet.

"He said he couldn't wait any longer. He wanted to beat the rain."

Loretta ran to the water. As she ran, she shouted, "Ada! Ada! Ada! Don't forget your promise!"

Adam didn't turn. He didn't respond. She wasn't even sure if he had heard her. The Loretta Lynn just kept going further and further out to sea, the sound of the motor fading away.

A wave hit Loretta smack in the face, bringing her back to reality. At that point, she realized she was chest deep in the water. Feeling deflated and dejected, she waded back to shore, joining Calvin on the sand. He just stared at her.

"I couldn't find the rain cloak. I looked for it. I didn't find it," she told him as she looked out at the sea, lost.

"It's ok," he said.

As they walked back to the Marshall Yard compound, she started to cry. It didn't rain at all that day.

A Week Later

Adam had not called. Loretta began her teacher's training program.

A Month Later

Christmas came and went with no word from Adam. Loretta said there must be a valid explanation. Calvin agreed.

Three Months Later

Adam had not called or written. Captains, fishermen and other seafarers reported seeing a blue pirogue with a sole occupant, always a distance away from them. When they attempted to contact the vessel or get closer, the vessel always seemed to disappear.

Six Months Later

Adam's father suffered a heart attack and died. Calvin blamed Adam. He said their father died more of a broken heart. Loretta tried her best to console Calvin.

Nine Months Later

Loretta graduated from teacher's training. Calvin was there to celebrate the occasion with her and her mother. No word from Adam.

Loretta took a part time job at a grocery store. Calvin told her to consider letting Adam go.

"He has moved on Loretta. You should too."

"I still have hope. It's not a year yet."

Ten Months Later

Loretta's mother died. Calvin consoled her. He asked her to move into his and his brother's home in order to cut her expenses. She refused.

Eleven Months Later

Calvin begged Loretta to let his brother go and marry him.

"How can I Cally? You know I love Ada. There must be a reason we haven't heard from him. He will explain when he comes back."

"He goes away for a whole year, and you believe he's coming back with a valid explanation? He's out there somewhere doing God knows what. It's heartbreaking to see you suffer like this."

"As long as he's in my heart, it's not broken. And Calvin, even if I did let him go, why would you think I would, or should be with you?"

One Year Later

"No. I didn't hear from him. Nobody's heard. But I know he's not coming back. Not today. Not anytime. He's not coming back. He's ..."

"Calvin, what are you talking about?" When Loretta looked at him, she saw the same hopeless look she saw in his eyes a year ago in that same spot.Tears welled up in his eyes, again. "He's not coming back because he's dead. He's dead because I killed him. Loretta, I killed Adam."

Loretta let out a raucous "HA!" A sound so loud and wild that it caught Calvin off guard. Just as quickly, the laugh disappeared and was replaced by one of rage. She walked forcefully towards him, like a soldier in drill.

"You!" She shouted at him, while poking her index finger up at his face. "Ever since Adam left, and even before that, you have been trying to get between us. To get at me,"

Loretta screamed at him. It was the first time that Calvin, or anyone else for that matter, had seen Loretta angry.

"You've envied what we have and you would do anything to break us up. To say something like that is just low. But you can't, because what we have is real, and...."

"Let me guess," Calvin interrupted. "Real love is not measured by the amount of time you spend together. It's measured by the amount of time you can spend apart and still love like if you're together, right?"

"Yes!"

"Funny," Calvin said, shaking his head. "Those were his last words."

"Last words?" her tone softer now. "What do you mean?"

"Loretta, remember when you went for the rain cloak?"

"Yes."

Although he was speaking to Loretta, Calvin now had the attention of the everyone on the beach.

One Year Earlier

"Loretta, could you do me the favour and run for it please? I could give my farewell lecture and hug to my brother in the meantime."

"OK. Sure. I'll be right back."

As Loretta made her way off the beach, the brothers both stared at her leaving.

"Stop drooling big brother." Adam laughed and gave Calvin a playful nudge with his elbow." "Your eyes will fall out."

"You have to be the stupidest little brother in the world," big brother said in a scolding voice. "How you could leave a woman like Loretta on her own will go down as the biggest mistake man ever made, after that ass ate the apple from his wife. It must be an Adam thing."

"Don't worry Cally. We've got this. What we have is about trust and real, true love. There isn't anything that could come between that. Plus, I know you will look out for my interest."

"You're going to break her heart. You're going to go to Trinidad, meet some nice Indian girl and bring her back and show her off. Or, as soon as you turn your back she is going to turn hers. Either way, I promise you, in one year's time, this isn't going to end well."

The brothers debated back and forth briefly about the possibilities from this trip: Adam spoke of the pros. Calvin, the cons. Apart from their views on the outcome, the two boys were not much different ideologically and physically. Besides the two-year age difference and about a two-inch height advantage for Calvin, Adam was darker due to the time spent outdoors, and more muscular from the strenuous work. Calvin was the careful one. Adam, obviously, was the risk taker.

Calvin suggested they put the Loretta Lynn to sea. Adam hopped aboard, positioning himself at the stern, started the motor, letting it throttle quietly as the motor warmed up. The stern faced the beach, the bow pointing seaward. Calvin got on board, sat facing Adam and said, "Little brother, I just want you to know that when you're gone, I will take the best care of her. When you get back, she will be your sister-in-law. I promise you."

Adam was enraged. "I see the way you look at her, Calvin. You wish it were you she was looking at. You still can't have her though, because what we have is true love. Even when we're apart, we still love as if we are together."

Calvin leaned forward and spoke harshly. "Someday, little brother, your words will be repeated all over the world by foolish lovers." As he spoke, he grabbed a utility knife that was on the seat next to him and rammed it though the old army jacket that his brother was wearing. As he twisted the handle the way one turns a key after inserting it into a lock, he said, "She will be mine. It's a pity you won't be around to see it, though."

Adam opened his mouth but no words came. He just stared at his brother, confused. He slumped forward in pain and resignation. And in doing so, rested on the throttle, which moved Loretta Lynn forward. Calvin tried , but was unable to retrieve the knife. He barely managed to jump from the boat as it slowly motored out to sea. He waded to shore and once on the beach he turned to watch Loretta Lynn pick up pace.

Just then, Loretta McIntosh arrived at his side.

One Year Later

"And that's why he didn't wait. Because he couldn't wait. That's why he didn't look back. Because he couldn't look back. He was dead, Loretta. Gone."

Loretta was dumbstruck.

Calvin stooped down, his head in his hands. The crowd murmured.

Then they heard it before they saw it. A humming, revving sound out on the water.

"Who is that?" a bather asked.

"Somebody's coming," another said. "Look!"

Loretta and Calvin knew that familiar sound. It could only be the Loretta Lynn. It could only mean one thing: Adam has come back.

"But how?" Calvin asked, as he fell flat on his bottom, waves washing around him. "It can't be," he said. Eyes wide open. Mouth open wider.

The boat was still a ways out, approaching slowly. A single silhouette against an orange, setting sun. Loretta's emotions were playing games with her. Triumph. She knew he would come back. Anger. She couldn't believe Calvin would test her, and play such a cruel joke on her. Confusion. She wondered if Adam was involved in it. All her questions will be answered soon, she thought.

She moved over to where Calvin sat. She smiled and scolded him at the same time. "You are bad, Cally. Bad joke".

"It's not. It's not a joke. It can't be." His expression of horror didn't change. Loretta couldn't understand.

Somebody shouted, "Oh God!" joined by gasps from others. One woman wailed as she ran from the beach.

The vessel stopped when it ran aground on the beach. Loretta went numb when she beheld the horror that everyone else saw.

Into My Bloodstream Part 1

The day before I met you, I swore
I would love no more.
Twenty-four hours later
I couldn't get enough of you.
Yes, It's true!
What a difference a day makes.

You were into me.
You made me wait to get into you.
"Be patient," you said.
"I am patient," I said.
But when we met, when we touched,
Into my bloodstream you went.
Maybe it's im-patient I meant.

Before I met you, I swore
I'll hurt no more.
But I've been hurting ever since.

I bleed you.
I sweat you. I cry you.

But when I cry, you cry.
We cry. Together.
Tears well spent.

When we touched,
You poured into my pores
Into my bloodstream you went.

Into My Bloodstream Part 2

I've tried to read you,
But your body language is foreign,
Like a book written in Arabic, Russian, or Mandarin.
Oh, how I would love to turn your pages!
I look into your eyes,
You make my soul blush.
Your peace, your calm, make my adrenaline rush.
You smile. I laugh.
Your lips invite me to bare teeth.
Your voice caresses my earlobes whenever they meet.
We touch
And my spirit takes you in Like a nutrient.
Into my bloodstream you go.

Am I less of a man if I submit to you?
Go where you want me to go.
Do what you want me to do?
You rub my lamp like a genie
When you want me to come,
To fulfill all your wishes,
Your every desire.
At first there was resistance,
But as time told...
It no longer matters what you require.
I saw you as a hard task.
"Challenge accepted," I said.
But to you, I was no contest.
You had me tapping out instead.
I have lost all control to you, or so it may seem
But that's the way I would have it
As long as you remain in my bloodstream.

What Are You to Me?

My Best Friend My Soul Mate My Promise My Pal
My Confidant My Mentor My Everything My All
My Now and Forever
My Tea, Breakfast and Dinner My Comforter
My Counsellor
My Spiritual Advisor

My Love My Lover My Hands My Feet
My Alpha My Omega My Justice My Peace

My Baby My Honey
My Sunshine My Queen
My Yesterday My Tomorrow
My Everything In Between

God put all these in one soul
And came up with you
Then gave you to me
Proven, devoted and true

Mother's Dey

Aye Mammy! Yo dey?
Me good too. I dey here
Well, today is your dey
An' me just come fo wish yo Happy Mother's Dey!
Me war yo kno'
Me luv yo
An' me tank yo fo mekking me
An' fo putting up wid me all dem years.

Mammy, me tank yo fo all the cut backside yo gimme
Well, nah all, but some
Yo insistence on discipline
Yo advice an' all dem "ole people say" tings
Yo use to tell me
Me does quote yo plenty.

Anyway
Me bring yo some flowers from Floral Expressions
Fo de table vase
Some fruits; me kno' yo luv yo bananas
Some cupcakes from Daily Treats
Me kno' yo luv yo sweets
An a lickle hundred dollars
Me kno' yo love yo money too
Me go come back next week fo see yo agen, yo hear?
Me luv yo
Me gone.

Chronicles of a Woman Out of Love

She says she's not heartless, she's just using her heart less. She's been hurt a lot, so, she hurts a lot.

She doesn't care anymore because she cared before. And where did it get her?

Years of tears.

Trapped in a so-called relationship, the abuse only made her stronger.

Strong enough to abandon ship.

Good thing she didn't stay any longer.

She picked herself up, dusted herself off, pulled herself together, kept pushing.

Now she's looking forward to a better cycle, not menstrual. She decides to do what's best for her, that's mental.

Relationships are painful, so, she has mastered the painless art of "friends with benefits", and "likes and prefer", "one-night stands", and "boom, bam; thank you sir."

She has hurt a lot of feelings.

She remembers when she had feelings.

Now, she breaks hearts like wind – naturally. She comes and goes leaving men's hearts flailing in the wind – quite naturally.

She's the definition of the new Independent Woman that you may know: created by Destiny's Child and explained masterfully by Neyo.

She is asked, "What's the recipe?" She answers, with tears in her eyes, "Beware of the pretenders. Look out for the lies. Get your money. Meet your ends. Don't make enemies. Watch who you call friends. Be honest with yourself. True love does not exist. No means no. Trust God. That should have been first on the list. Use those precious gems, and make your own path. And do whatever it takes to protect your heart."

In Defense of My Friend Karmalita

They say Karma is a bitch, but I think she's a lady.
When I say that in certain circles,
Certain circles say I'm crazy.
Why?
Because I like to see people get their just desserts?
No, they say, because when she comes around,
Somebody always gets hurt.
Well, duh!
They must have done something bad sometime back;
If you're not paying it forward,
Then prepare for the pay back.
That's when Karma steps in.
What goes around comes around.
We can always choose our actions,
But we can't always choose the outcome.

They say Karma is a bitch, but I beg to disagree.
Karma says "What you want for you, give it to me."
Don't mistake her for her cousin Revenge.
He's a choice of action.
He's a plan, a plot, a strategy, a quest for satisfaction.
But Karma is a result of the alignment of mind and soul.
Karma is warm and just.
Revenge is just served cold.
You can be bitter, vengeful and angry
For the wrong that was done.
You can exact what you believe is justice.
A victory is won.
Or, you can be patient and calm,
And watch Karma do her thing;
It might take some time, but watch and see.
Guaranteed, refreshing.

They say Karma is a bitch, but I say they're one-sided.
We hear there's more sides to every story,
So by that we should be guided.

Karma stays in her humble abode.
She only comes out when activated,
When she hears the pleas and prayers
Of the innocent and violated,
The widow and the fatherless,
The indigent and poor,
Misused and abused,
Conned and despised,
Those loved no more.
Then Karma steps in and puts balance to the equation.
She's fair and upright, precise and on time,
True in every situation.

They say Karma is a bitch,
But I believe she's a blessing in disguise.
To the fool, just a bit of rotten luck,
But a lesson to the wise.
She teaches us to be reasonable, responsible, and caring.
Truthful, honest, friendly, forthright and endearing.

We could be cruel and crude,
Harmful, callous and crass,
Arrogant and haughty, a thorn in the side,
A downright pain in the ass.
However we choose to be in life, loving or unkind.
The choice is ours, but please remember,
She may not be far behind.

What's in a Name

Our foreparents was some kinda people.
It ain't funny;
When it did come to naming the place
Is like dey wanted to be remembered 'til eternity.
Everywhere dey went, dem put dem names:
Mr. George have ah town, Mr. Browne's got ah town,
Mr. Fairbairne have ah pasture, Mr. Calder have ah ridge,
Mr. Paul's got an avenue,
And Mr. Gordon have ah yard.
Dem put Miss Clare in de valley, Mr. Casson on de hill,
And leave Buddy and Georgie in de gutter.
Dem give Jackson ah bay, Lowmans ah bay,
Sandy ah bay, Miss Sally ah spring,
And only give Miss Yambou ah river.
Mrs. Wynne have ah mount, Mrs. Bentick have ah mount,
Oh, Miss Young have ah mount too.
Mr. Murray's got ah village,
Mr. Mc Kie's got ah hill, Mr. Reeve's got ah level
(with that I don't know what he going to do).
Miss Chester have ah cottage,
Miss Dasent have ah cottage,
Miss Rose have ah cottage, ah hall, ah bank, and ah place.
Mr. Langley had ah park, Mr. Ottley had ah hall,
And Mr. Akers had ah wide open space.
Yo know, yo go into ah region and because of de name,
You expect to see certain things.
But:
I pass through Bridgetown, I didn't see none.
I pass through Maroon Hill, I didn't see none.
I pass through Cherry Hill, I didn't see none.
I pass through Cedars, I didn't see none.
I didn't even see no new grounds in New Grounds!
Plan was disorganized.
Level Gardens was crooked. Chilli was hot.
Spring Village was dry. New Montrose was old.

Green Hill was brown!
There was
No guns in Trigger Ridge.
No cutlass in Choppins. No coals in Coulls Hill.
No rich man in Richmond Hill. No gold in Golden Vale.
No diamonds in Diamonds. No cane in Cane Garden.
And no beach in Glen!

Gladiate

This is no movie.
The blood, sweat, and tears are real.
And as they soak the sand where I sit, or stand or lie,
They reinforce where I am
And who I am.
Unceremoniously. Unjustly. Unwittingly
Tossed into a ring of hopeless madness
With hopeless madmen
Like myself,
Forced to fight for my right to see another day.
Everyday.
That's what I'm fighting for.
I fight against lies.
Lies perpetrated by unheard voices.
They batter and bruise my psyche and my reputation,
Or what's left of them.
I fight against jealousy.
Jealous ones still envy me
Despite the fact that at any moment I can be slain.
Jealous ones who envy what?
My indomitable spirit?
My resilience?
My wisdom? My Betty?
I'm fighting with nothing.
Nothing but my God-given defenses.
I'm belted up, booted up.
Chest plated. Helmeted. Shielded.
I yearn for a sword!
I'm fighting without fear though.
Without fear of what they may think
Or what they may say,
And despite what they may do.
I am a slave, a prisoner, a gladiator.
So, I'll fight until there's no more fight left to fight.
You are entertained, aren't you?
Of course.
That's why you're here.

Karl Telemaque

*Karl Telemaque is from the Grenadine island of Bequia.
A barber by profession, Karl also enjoys participating in sports and
of course, writing. He is a Sagittarius and describes himself as an
extrovert, generous, funny and optimistic.*

Why Is Thursday So Hot?

Why is Thursday so hot?
I have to wear a hat
I go the beach to cool the heat
In the shade I fall asleep
Why is Thursday so hot?

Why is Thursday so hot?
No rain is falling
Not a drizzle
I call on the rain
But it doesn't answer back
Why is Thursday so hot?

Why is Thursday so hot?
Seems the clouds forgot to form
The busy streets
The burning heat
It's global warming on the attack
Lord, why is Thursday so hot?

Why is Thursday so hot?
Maybe we ask that a lot
Must we forget the One
Responsible for that?

Why is Thursday so hot?
God made the world
The sun and the rain
He made the stars
And called each by their name
Whether it rains
Or whether it shines
I thank Him all the same
Amen.

Farewell My Love

Is it really true
Our love is over now?
Can it be time to say goodbye?
You're moving towards a new life without me?
I can't believe we really are going to part.
I'm left with scars upon my broken heart.
It's too soon.
Much too soon.
We shared our lives
And gave so much love.
But what can I say?
Go now if you must.
I'll get by.
I'll set you free without inducing guilt.
I don't want you to know
How much it hurts
But as you leave, silent tears will flow.
I can't be mad.
I'll hide my sadness.
Happiness is what I wish for you.
I hope that you fare well.

Farewell my love.

Jason Delpesche

Writing poetry is one of the many artistic skills that Jason possesses.
He also enjoys singing, dancing and acting and hopes some day that one
of these talents would bring him a breakthrough in entertainment.

Prison Life

It's waiting on letters
When you're doing time
And your family won't write
Or send you a dime.

It's waiting for visits
That never take place
From friends and loved ones
Who forget your face.

It's hearing them lying
And say that they're trying.

It's making plans with someone
You thought you knew;
Suddenly their plans change.
They don't include you.

It's hearing them say
How much they care;
But in time of need
They disappear.

It's hearing them make promises
That go straight to your head
But when push comes to shove
They push out instead.

It's expressing yourself to people
Who pretend to believe;
But they won't ever feel your pains,
So pains remain unrelieved.

It's calling and hearing
There's a block on the phone.
You must maintain composure
So life goes on alone.

It's really messed up
Doing prison time.
That's just prison life for you.
Out of sight, out of mind.

Don't Give Up

Don't give up and don't give in
It's all in God's hands.
No matter what you are facing
He is the one who can.
In any situation
His grace can turn it around.
You can be victorious
Because His love abounds.

He's the beginning and the end
And all that's in between.
Put your total trust in Him
Because to Him it's all foreseen.
He knows about your struggles
He knows about your pain.
Your hardships and your sorrows
He will help you to reign.

Don't give up
Don't quit before it's time.
God's grace will give you power
To make it to the finish line
In His way and in His time.

Jerome Ollivierre

Jerome Ollivierre was born on the beautiful Grenadine island of Mayreau. A water taxi operator by profession, Jerome enjoys meeting people, traveling, playing music and basketball. When he's not busy doing those things, he likes to immerse himself in a good book.

My Paradise

Picture perfect, I have to mention
The last unspoilt Grenadine island
1.5 square miles of beauty
350 Christian smiles to greet you
Surrounded by coral reef
White sand
Palm tree beaches
Restaurants and bars to fill your taste buds
Guitars and drums to entertain you
Fish, conch all year 'round
Lobster when in season

Snorkelling tours for your underwater sensation
Lots of beautiful fishes to see
Swim with turtles
Wow, this must be a movie

I assure you it is not.
IT IS NOT
This is real
This is Mayreau and the Tobago Cays
In the Cays you don't swim with the fishes
They swim with you
The turtles transport you to any of the five islands
Iguana posing for pictures
And conch walking on the sand

You think I done
You can visit Petite Tabak
Where they filmed scenes from "Pirates of the Caribbean"

Please when you're vacationing
Wear nothing but a smile
Take nothing but pictures
Leave nothing but footprints

Some say Myro
Others say Mayreau
For me it is simply home
This is my paradise

Ole People Say

Ole people say:
"Friends does carry yo, but dey doh bring yo back."
Dem sure right 'bout dat.
Imagine, I never wanted this
And now I have it
I doh war lose it.
After five years, I still doh know wat going happen to me.
I have all the other essentials,
Is best dem give me ah key.
You getting one hour everyday, to wash, exercise, etcetera.
It doh matter if sun shining, or if we have bad weather.
Dem say lunch time is fun time
That for me is the wuss time.
Occasionally, you get some 'sauce food'
But u better can swim.
I doh kno' way longer: that, or my time waiting.
But the meal of the day is rice and chicken.
The rice white, white, white,
Is either dem bleach it, or snow falling in the kitchen.
The chicken have so much colour
I believe the chef is ah ink master.
You in a cell with 30 other men.
For me is one eye close, and one eye open.
All is not lost
This is merely a pit stop.
So ah using me time constructively
I attending classes, from some I dun graduate
Plus ah get me certificate
So dat when ah go out
Ah ready for the place.

Taylor Mofford

Taylor Mofford hopes that her poetry and stories would encourage others not only to enjoy reading, but also to take an interest in writing. She aspires to become a published author in the near future.

Mark Me!

On a Saturday morning, not too long ago, standing ad-midst wind-swept garbage abandoned by sanitation work-ers, my stomach cramped, my nails dug into my palms. I flexed my fingers and turned my back to a glass door that, unlike water that lies hazily about defined matters, reflect-ed my malnourished body. I was tired of staring at my cracked skin and dull brown eyes. I hated that my lips, once full, were now chapped. My nose was the only thing that retained its glory, a perfectly straight remembrance of my mother's failure.

Everyone around town either knew my mother or had an idea of who she was. If I had to explain things in a very simple way, I'd just say she was another of the hopeless, pathetic crack heads you'd see cautiously limping by in arthritic pain, looking as though a tornado had passed though their lives.

Many claim that my mother was once a tall beauty with a thick afro. Thin lips, they said, but a welcoming smile that accompanied her alluring brown eyes. Some had long de-cided that her physique, which resembled that of a model, had a lot to do with the attention that was once lavished on her.

That was long before the men and the drugs.

If you inquire carefully, people will mostly remember my mother as she was before she died of a drug overdose: the scars that disfigured her body, the AIDS that sucked her dry because she refused her medication, the six good teeth that remained among rotting ones, and the centipede-like scar that made her left eye significantly different from the right. Eyes, they'll remember, that had lost their glow, and were replaced with hopelessness. And if you would have dared to ask about her children, you'd be burdened by the stories you'd hear of the first boy named John who followed in his mother's footsteps and was now a fifteen year old, disrespectful crack head. And if you inquire a bit further, you'd know that boy is me.

*   *   *

The honk of a horn brought me back, painfully, to the uncaring hustlers who busied themselves pushing carts and trollies, the mothers tugging on hands of nagging little boys and girls, crack heads laughing at apparitions, begging for dollars they believed they deserved, while self-dignified vagrants pulled their pants above their navels with one hand and reached out with the other for a shadow of wealth.

Across the street, Short Man tried to convince the busy people of Kingstown that the bag of mangoes in his hand was the last one, and they should either buy it or lose out on a golden opportunity. Mr. Grey, who owned the supermarket where Short Man had set up business, stopped and briefly discussed something with Short Man before he glanced in my direction. I was in a recumbent position on the second step that led to the mockery of a vegetable market reeking of stale urine and rotten fruits.

Polite people normally did this funny thing sometimes: they looked at me from different angles without directly looking at me, so I wouldn't think they were staring. It had long become a normal thing. I was used to the cross eyes as much as I was to the baneful expressions.

Mr. Grey had crossed eyes that morning. I forced a smile and painfully waved at him. I knew he just wanted to ensure that I was doing well in spite of.

There was a tap on the top of my head. I scrambled nervously to my feet and came face to face with a thick giant of a woman who had sweat running down her forehead and into her almost black, bold eyes. "I knew your mother," she said.

It took only the mention of my mother and my need for a hit to make my head start pounding.

"I knew your mother," she repeated. "She had hopes that her children would be better off than she was." She tugged on the straps of her leather handbag and shoved it up her shoulder.

"I remember one time you came to visit her at the prison and she was so excited to see you although you brought bad news." She reached for me like my mother would have, and it raised goose bumps on my skin. I stepped back and either she didn't notice or she didn't care.

She went on, "Your mother was happy and furious at the same time, and I couldn't help but wonder how it was possible. I saw in that moment a hopeless mother. She said the elder boys and men at the St. Georges Home For Boys, where you were, kept doing things to you that they shouldn't."

Memories came roaring back.

I'm standing in Mr. B's room with tears and snot running towards my chin. The air stinks of stale cigarettes and strong rum.

A lizard eases its way cunningly towards a spider that hangs from the crooked frame of a picture of Nelson Mandela. The bed is unmade. None of the boys have been barked at as yet to be slaves. On the mahogany table placed tastelessly in the center of the room are three of our greatest fears as boys of the twisted home: condoms, strong rum and a thick strap rumored to be soaked weekly in stale piss.

The strong rum is mostly feared. (There are times you'd collect a strap over your back for no apparent reason other than Mr. B's drunkenness.) The condoms are another story all by themselves.

"I don't care for a Nike or a Jordan Mr. B," I am shouting. "I only care for a shoe that doesn't have a tongue."

"Worthless pieces of shit don't get the opportunity to choose what they want, John." He turns to face me while spitting venom in my direction as he reaches for a pack of condoms and draws closer to me.

"Your mother is a piece of shit. You're a piece of shit, and I'm going to make sure you're not forgetting that."

My breath catches in my throat for a second and I mentally decide not to give him the satisfaction he craves. I stand my ground not flinching.

I fought through the unpleasant memories and came back to a very strange question that pushed me closer to the edge.

Giant Lady was tapping the sweat away with a handkerchief that had seen better days.

"Do you know what our biggest flaw as poverty-stricken humans is, John?" Giant Lady asked.

My stomach clenched. A cold sweat broke out above my cracked lips and forehead. My patience thinned. All I really wanted was a hit.

"Ignorance boy," she bellowed in the midst of the crowded city. "Ig-nor-ance," she repeated in a whisper, parsing the word on her lips. My anger rose. I was fed up hearing the same thing over and over again from people who approached me in the streets.

Bitterness choked me.

"Chicks have mothers," I said. "Pigs have mothers. Hell, even rats and cockroaches have mothers, but I have never had a mother a day in my life. I had a child donor. A child donor!" I screamed. My frustration rose in volumes.

I was itching for a fight, and all she could do was stand there and give me advice. I needed money. I needed a fix!

"And what did she care to donate to this world?" I dragged my hands over my tattered Pokémon shirt that was once white but was now black from my grimy life. "A piece of shit."

Giant Lady stared at me with wonder, as though she couldn't believe my level of self-degradation. I turned around and made my way towards The Slum, forgetting my manners. I didn't say goodbye.

The road to Paul's Avenue, better known as Paul's Lot or The Slum, passed the high court and Everest Trading captured the meaning of the word slum. There were old carts and tables scattered on both sides of the road. Garbage took flight into people's homes. Houses begged to be repaired. Naked children ran up and down the rat-infested streets, while mothers screamed at them to get their asses out of the road.

A few buildings down, a police officer complained loudly and unprofessionally to anyone who cared to listen about having to stand in the blazing sun. He tried to appear intimidating in order to deter outlaws from serious crimes such as murder and rape, as well as petty ones like throwing contraband over the prison's walls. I fixed the pouch that was attached to my ripped jeans, stared straight ahead, hands at my side like a Nutcracker Man, and walked on towards The Spaniard's.

"Some things are better left alone," I told myself.

The Spaniard was a lanky, middle-aged man with unusually thick hair and eyebrows. The junkies speculated he smoked as much as he dealt, maybe even twice as much, which was probably the reason for his gauntness. He was not to be messed with. Nobody really knew why he was called "The Spaniard," and no one dared to ask.

He was sitting in the rocking chair on his porch counting dollars and cents in a tall jar. I walked up to him and cleared my throat nervously.

I placed a twenty-dollar bill on the porch railing and was rewarded with his attention. Money talks, bullshit walks was forever the motto.

My stomach growled, reminding me I needed a meal; my palms were sweating and my fingers were twitching, reminding me I needed a hit.

I collected two rocks, tucked them away in my crotch from prying hands of the older and stronger smokers and made my way to the back yard. I sat as comfortably as I could in a corner of the Spaniard's yard where you weren't ever vilified for the path you chose. People actually understood that people fall, and though they fall they weren't beyond recovery. The issues of hunger weren't trivialized by the well-fed people. The scent of sex hung in the air.

With a cigarette cocked at the corner of my lips, I hit the tip with trembling fingers and awaited the ashes for my gun. Hungrily, I removed one of the mini balls from my crotch and unfolded the foil to reveal my addiction -- a tiny piece of crack that resembled the sugary part of my grandmother's groundnut sugar cake.

My stomach did a somersault that instantly made me feel as though I needed to go off. I placed the ash and the crack on the pipe and steadied my breath while I lit the tip of my addiction.

I knew my high was seconds away as it frizzled and popped. I inhaled with all my might. My mood depended on this. My ears rang as I held in the smoke, then swallowed in gulps and waited for the bubble in my head.

I sat wide eyed for a minute, as people shuffled around with blank stares seeking their own addictions. Some instantly changed personalities. Some became bacchanalist, some acrobats, some exorcists. This was the moment I had been waiting for: the high was beginning. This was what it was all about.

I chuckled at the pandemonium as the screaming in my ears ceased little by little. I pulled the other and went up again, through images of charging soldiers with guns and bellows. Short Man was walking purposefully towards me with no idea in the world that if he didn't increase his pace, he would be trampled.

I fought against the urge to violently hold Short Man and the soldiers off.

"They're not really there," I whispered to myself.

"Off with their heads," my Chief Demon shouted.

I felt like I was running towards the soldiers as I inhaled again. Somewhere within me I knew the scene unfolding before me was a hallucination, but I couldn't tell that to my brain.

Perhaps I was as worthless as they said, or maybe it was the crack that messed it all up for a young, swarthy boy, or just maybe it was my Mother who created all the hopelessness for me. But whatever it truly was, it always boiled down to my worthlessness and my mother. Everything always seemed to go right back to my mother, something like a generational curse.

Short Man ran his fingers through his jet-black Indian hair gelled in spikes atop his head. He had small delicate features and a fine voice I knew would be gone in a matter of time to be replaced with a raspy one. He held out a plastic bag with what appeared to be more than a month's salary worth of crack wrapped in foil.

It was automatic, like the way the touch or sight of water tends to make you want to urinate. My stomach tugged, and my fingers twitched at the sight of my addiction. I had finally caught the thing that was eluding me: a greater high.

Short Man sat cross-legged across from me and took his pipe from the waistband of his boxers. He stared at me and I read his need in his eyes. Words were not necessary.

We smoked round after round. We smoked our surroundings into wild hallucinations. My head felt light. My vision blurred momentarily. Our eyes were bulging red.

While inhaling my tenth shot, I heard the Methodist Church bell chiming the arrival of twelve o'clock, and just like that, Cinderella images started appearing. I lost focus of everything around me and tumbled forward. In the distance, there came the thump of slight receding footsteps. The last thing I saw was a blurry vision of Short Man's Nike.

I came back to blinding lights that weren't heavenly. IV fluids were running through my veins. Mushy limbs and an empty bedside. Short Man was not around. Two beds down, a bulky doctor was pointing in my direction with an unbothered expression. The nurse he gave instructions to shuffled her thick limbs towards me.

"We're discharging you," she said without looking at me.

"I'm not feeling well."

"Doctor's instructions. He needs the bed for a politician's son." Gently, she took the drips from my right hand. "Don't say I told you though."

For some strange reason I wasn't surprised. Who would want a piece of shit like me to occupy a good bed that was needed for good people.

Unexpectedly, she looked at me and smiled. "You'll be fine," she said. "God takes care of His children in this evil world."

An hour later, I walked out of the hospital with a hundred-dollar bill given to me by a kind soul and went right back into the yard of The Spaniard.

One week later, there is still no sunshine in my life. There are still winter days, and it's cold and dreary.

Now, if you take one minute to care, you'll see that I am still in that tattered Pokémon shirt and ripped jeans. I am not sitting in a classroom at age fifteen. There's no confidence surging through me. I do not walk with ambitious children of tomorrow.

I am still that disrespectful crack head sleeping on the street at age fifteen, grabbing at ladies' purses and their butts, and receiving my share of slaps. I haven't yet arrived at the point where I decide that I will not allow another person to touch me in places that make my stomach crawl and threaten me beyond tears.

I am still blamed solely for my mother's lack of parenting skills. Nobody seems to acknowledge where they went wrong. It seems as though they don't know that they have committed infanticide — they killed the child in me, and they don't care that I was once a child with a lot of moxie.

Crack is still my best friend, and there is no fight left in me to defend myself against this thing that whispers beautiful promises of a family and a home.

Today, I am curled in a ball of disappointment on the almost soaked pavement of the supermarket compound, away from the bustling crowd. Nobody is staring now and calling me names. I am tired of the abuse. I am tired of the degrading looks. I have no fight left in me to scream, "Remove those eyes! Remove those eyes! My mother's mistakes are not my own!"

I curl myself tighter and try to shut out the violent commands in my head, and on that cold pavement I whisper and let the wind carry my words to the people of my homeland:

"Mark me! Mark me for the person I aspire to be one day. Mark me for a better me!"

Dahlia's Summer

Another summer passed
A remarkable one
Your sugar-laced smile pierced me
Foolishly, I looked up to you
God must have been disappointed

I laid bare for you
For your roaming hands
Your throbbing possession-erect passion
You explored me irresponsibly
As you tormented my pure soul
Bared before you

You scattered seeds
In my greenhouse
You thought yourself a man
I thought you to be charming

We planted a flower together
Hopes of a garden blossomed in my mind
After serious contemplations
Scenes of golden-spiked lies
I knew you'd never meant to stay

I watched helplessly
As our love trekked in different directions
After such a memorable summer

Not knowing any better
I was just an innocent teenager
You a seasoned one

You left your flower to the wind
Unattended
You paid no further attention to its cultivation
I thought you knew
Planting to be a progressive process

Weeds grew up
Threatened to choke our Dahlia
Summer after summer
I watered and nurtured our Dahlia

You should see our flower now
Our now nineteen-year-old Dahlia
I'd like to think
She compliments us both

I promised myself though,
Two memory-filled summers ago
That Dahlia would never
Be innocently a charmer.
Someone like her irresponsible father

Not My Master

You are not the master of my life.
I am not to be had.
I AM OF VALUE!
I refuse to be told otherwise.
Give me a second
I must convince my heart
Tell it of reasons to flee from your deceit.
You vitrify my heart
Then shatter it to pieces.
Please
Just give me a second.
I must convince myself
That your love is vitally important.
Or is it your hate?
You continuously take my breath away.
Hit me
Do it one more time
My screams have made you powerful, eh?
Your hands dancing across my flesh
With great vitality.
It ends now, you hear?
I promised my mother I'd stay and work it out,
Figure it out,
Have it sorted out.
There's no doubt now
I'm walking out.
I am paving my own way you hear?
Starting a brand-new day, you hear?
Stretching towards the light, you hear?
Leaning towards what's right, you hear?
You're not the master of my life, YOU HEAR?
I will fight.
I WILL FIGHT!!

This is my series of pithy declarations.

I have blocked out
Your vociferous demands.

Cease fire!
I just thought I'd let you know.

We

In Vincy we do things differently
See we in we undies
You see we?
We dutty eh?
We happy though
Pitching marbles, picking mangoes
You know hopscotch?
You know one, two, three red light?
Fine mannequins we as kids
Does mek right?
You think we can't stuff plastic bags
With bush to play rounders?
Watch how we creative in we undies
Hear the bamboo dem blow!
Eyebrows get bun off
We don't pay that no mind though
Grass done scratch up we skin
From playing coopee
We in we undies
We happy
You see we?

Dream World

In you I take
One step forward.
Fear becomes a stranger,
Weakness becomes a foe.
In you I feel completely invincible.
You take me beyond my shattered pieces.
I fly
Over crimson stains of embarrassment
That spread beyond my reach.
I trample upon roaring lions
And poisonous serpents.
I am powerful now.
I will not bend.
I am here now.
I will not shatter.
In this world of perfection,
My heart is the only thing you hold dear.
Do you see reason?
Will you listen now?
Now that I am invincible in a dream,
I wish was a reality.

Alana Hudson

Alana Hudson migrated to St. Vincent and the Grenadines in 2002 where she obtained her primary and secondary education. She graduated from the Bishop College Secondary School, Kingstown earning a certificate in Business Studies as well as the prestigious Student of the Year award in 2014. She further attained an Associate Degree in Fine Arts, Design and Cultural Communication at the SVG Community College. Passionate about art, Alana is a talented painter and skilled art designer.

Adolescence

So, what if I got drunk
Smoked 'til I was high
Partied all weekend
Not caring how much I spent?

So, what if I didn't care
About your advice
And hooked up with strangers
Without thinking twice?

And what if I told you now
I wish I had listened to your counsel.
Alas! Here I am
In this penitentiary.

You spoke from experience.
I acted out of defiance
Young and foolish
Not thinking about consequences
Never knowing people were fake and pretentious.

So, what if I said I'm sorry?
I feel like another burden you have to bear.
So, what if I said I would make you proud again?
Would you care?
I've learned my lesson because of this.
Things will be different.

I promise!

Misunderstood Struggles

Many see me and think they understand me.
Ha ha ha. What a joke!
At one point
I thought I understood me, too.
It's becoming really easy to hide my feelings with a smile
And laughter that only lasts for a while.
Everyone seems to think all is well,
But what I keep inside I'll never tell.

These monsters make me believe this is comfort.
The sight of blood suppresses the emotional hurt.
These monsters keep fighting me, tempting me,
Screaming at me, "START CUTTING! START CUTTING!"

A cut here, a stab there.
They make me hit myself too,
Until I'm black and blue.
It's becoming a struggle.
Once again I prepare for battle.

I try to push these thoughts away;
In my mind I pray they would stay.
Thankfully, I'm on a mission to be a better person.
I'm alive for a reason
And I want to show the world
That I'm more than just a pretty girl.

My Saviour

Whenever I feel down
The best expression on my face is a frown —

When it seems I'm fascinated with what's on the floor
And I tell myself
I can't take this anymore —

That's when He holds my hand
And the angels help me
To withstand all of life's obstacles
And open my eyes to His miracles.

I'm never alone when He is around.
With Him I stand on solid ground.
My burdens He freely takes
And His love for me He never fakes.

He's my best friend.
Faithful 'til the end.
My refuge and fortress
In my times of distress.

I fall to my knees to unload all my stress.

Caswell Smart

*Caswell Smart is no stranger to the literary arts.
He has composed dozens of poems
and hopes to become a recording artiste
and a minister of religion.*

Slaves Enslaving Slaves

I saw it!
Slaves enslaving slaves,
Men spiting men of their own race.
I saw prisoners locking prisoners up
Shutting them in like pigs!

I saw it!
I tell no lie!
Men doing the work of law enforcers
Just to get ranks in the Babylonish system!

I saw it!
Prisoners insulting prisoners
For a piece of bread,
Forgetting that they themselves are prisoners.

I am a prisoner.
It is a system like hell.
I ask myself:
Will slavery ever end?

Free Me!

I am locked in
Free me!
The bars are real
Free me!
The bars are everywhere
Come free me!
My very soul screams for redemption.
Come now
Save me!
My patience is running out.

Come quickly
Free me!
This cell is like hell,
It's odious fumes I smell.
If you don't rescue me,
It's a story I won't tell

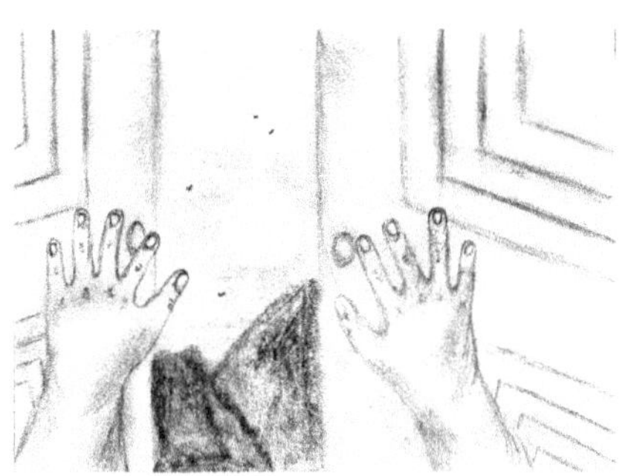

The chains are heavy
Come save me!
They are too tight,
They are hurting me!

Sins bind me intentionally,
But by Your power,
By Your greatness,
Set me free from prison,
Yes, from hell,
This prison of sin.

Remanded

Remanded in prison,
Another of life's lessons
Teaching me wisdom and humility.
My faith's getting stronger
As I place my trust
In the almighty God, Jehovah.

Time is passing.
It seems they are taking too long.
It's been six plus years!
I'm waiting,
Waiting to hear:
"You are free to go."

I am remanded,
Yes, remanded.
My courage gets stronger every second
While my patience wears thin.
I wait to be free again
To walk the streets of liberty again!

Lucresha Nanton

Born and raised in the village of Owia on the beautiful Caribbean island of St. Vincent in St. Vincent and the Grenadines, Lucresha is a former registered nurse who still has a passion to care for others. She considers her family and her Christian faith most important in her life. She enjoys doing embroidery work, unearthing good poetry, curling up in bed with a good book, and spending time with family and a few friends.

Unfaithful

My mind is tormented
With images of skilful hands caressing silky skin
Skin that should have only been mine to caress.
Your thirsty mouth on his
Devouring with relentless hunger
The essence of madness
Passion I hadn't seen in years

How could I ever forget
Thunderous raindrops pounding on galvanized roof
Scandalous candles casting hurtful reflections
Through his dark room
The travelling scents of lavender and honey
  as they filled the air
Your smooth arching back shimmering in
  illuminated candlelight
Like a goddess sent from the heavens above
Long flowing hair,
Dark as the midnight sky
Plump lips red as the blood in my veins

I should have known
That what I gave you wasn't enough.
Weren't my calloused hands skilful enough ?
Did I deliver pain in the place of pleasure?
Did I not travel deep enough
To your innermost being?
Was it all fake?
All pretence?
The moans?
The groans?

How could I have been so naïve,
Misled by your ability to manipulate?
Now, you smile.
My whole world shatters

My lovely wife
Love of my life
This deceptive devil in disguise
How, oh how, could you betray me?

An Aunty's Love

I love my aunty dearly
My favorite aunt in the whole wide world!
I love the yummy smell of pancakes and bacon
Flooding through my room.
I love how she spoiled me rotten.
She buys me the best shoes, clothes and snacks.
I love stealing her gummy bears
And laughing 'til my belly feels like exploding
When she comes with her tickle attacks.
We would eat our favorite ice cream
Slide and swing at Salt Pond park
Then stuff ourselves with food and juice.
I miss the comfort of falling asleep in her arms on the couch.
She always knows how to make me smile
And helps me with my homework.
My Aunty.
My Hero.
I love you!

Inner Turmoil

I feel the pain surge through me
As my heart breaks.
To get rid of this feeling
I'd do whatever it takes.

To quiet the screams
I hear in my head,
Just one day of joy
I beg instead.

I never knew
I could hurt this deeply.
I never knew
Every day I could be sad and weepy.

Please God,
Take away my pain
So I can finally wake up
To a brighter day.

Seasons of Change

My mind is always racing
I miss my lovely home
Being stuck in this wretched prison
I might as well be in a dome
Some days I don't want to wake up
Some days I can't help but cry
Other days are filled with laughter
Thank God for my friends inside

I hear sorrow in my mother's voice
How she fakes joy but fears for my life
It's prison so she assumes the worst.
And when asked if I'm ok
I always answer, "Of course."
I try to comfort her in any way I can
Looking forward to the day I can hold her hand
Since this wretched encounter with the law
And I felt all hope was lost
I renewed my faith in Jesus Christ
Cause this has to get better, at all costs
As I go through the next season of my life
I know I will be okay
Because I know all things are possible
With God by my side
This may be my season of sorrow
And weeping may endure for the night
But since joy cometh in the morning
I know I will be alright

Reynold Roberts

*Reynold comes from Richland Park, Mesopotamia,
the "bread basket" of St. Vincent and the Grenadines.
He has held many jobs in the hospitality industry,
and has worked at a few five-star resorts
around the Caribbean. He enjoys all genres of music,
speaks three languages and aspires to be a novelist.
He hopes that his pieces would be enjoyed by all.*

My Time

My time will come,
When I will shine
Bright like the sun
My time will come

Fears and obstacles in my way
Sitting, waiting, counting the days.
Time is my enemy
Time is my friend

I close my eyes,
Pondering the whys
Keeping my wits alert
Even though my days are dark

My time will come
Thinking of my son
Waiting for this to end
My time will come

Reminiscing on love
As it takes flight like a dove
Dark thoughts abate
Sense of well-being deflates

My time will come
Plans are made in spite of
As things turn to just stuff
My time will come

Dread develops
Darkness envelops
Everything comes undone
Time has won

Needle Immorality

Watching it long and limp,
She moistens her lips
With an intent look in her eyes --
She is undaunted by the size.

As she takes it in trembling hands
She guides it to her mouth
Takes her first lick
But it falls out with a flick.

She tries again
And sticks it deep within.
Her tongue strokes it wet like rain
But frustration begins to set in.

Irritated, she pulls it out.
There it stands, erect.
Again, she takes it to her mouth.
She's glad that she's adept.

With a sense of satisfaction
She guides it to the hole
But misses with a delayed action
Upset, her body runs cold.

Again, she tries
Sweat runs down her spine
It is thick with slime.
She hopes she gets it in this time.

Her mouth quivers,
As it slides in smoothly
Her body shivers
Supreme satisfaction, truly.

Now that this is done
Such a great relief!
It's hard to believe
Threading a needle can be such fun!

Sheba Charles

*Sheba Charles hails from Union Island/Vermont,
St. Vincent and the Grenadines. Her favorite color is blue.
Inspiration stems from her overactive imagination,
prison and uncertain feelings. She loves her dad loads
and loves Coppa D. Don even more.*

Dancing on the Clouds

Hey, we're gonna visit the skies tonight
Making it rain on everyone beneath us.
Turn off the lights, here we go!
Strawberry kisses ever so slight, mmm succulent.
Sweat glistens as morning dew
Oooh, hush now!

In this storm I'm gonna be your shelter.
Gentle whispers urge racking convulsions.
Bodies grating ignite our flame.
Simmer now.
Simmer down.
The curve of your spine brings me all in.

My lover, where there are scratches, there are bites.
I'm sure to earn some bragging rights.
We'll talk in thongs, dirty cuz we're in private.
You are burnt in my memory,
Screaming, moaning, sighing.
I light your fire to keep me warm
Dripping wet — don't turn off the faucet.
You're spent? Don't worry, I'll pay.
Open your eyes, see what we've done
We've danced on the clouds and made it rain.

Infatuated

I think I'd like to love you.
Nothing I'd usually go for but...
When I see you
My heart is in my throat
Palms start to sweat
My mind goes on a trip
Can't stop biting my lip
My face is hot

Ugh!
Flesh between my legs tingles,
Hating that I might have someone.
You're gonna be mine.
When you are, I'll stroke, lick,
Kiss you a thousand times.
I don't want to be friends.
We can cuddle in our warmth instead.
I'll trace your every outline
Drowning in your sexy-as-hell aura.
Oh my, you excite me!
I'm the drink and you're the chaser.

I tell you 'cause I want you to know
I'm in love with your skin, your intelligent eyes,
   your sly smirk,
The peeking chest tattoo.
Let me hold my composure.
What I wanna say is
I'll give you something to run to, not through.
I'd like to love you.
Would you like to love me too?

Fwen

So we good?
Whatever you're with, I'm with
I'm on what you're on
Ain't nobody gonna play with you when I'm with you
What's mine is yours

Hey Fwen, I need you
I poured out my heart
You had a drink
Now I cry tears, bleeding
My heart scorched
Oh how my stomach boils
Fwen, Fwen, is you doing me this?
You took my love, now you're gone?
You've trampled on my mind
Ever so often
Can't we work this out?
I see now
I hear you
Ok then
Our happiness was just an illusion
We were just a figment of my imagination
All that's left is sadness and confusion, Fwen?
I see
There's no prosperity here
You've turned your head
I get it
I didn't know any better
You lied
Why do you have to lie?
I see now
Prosperity has many friends
I have none
Real friends turn up in times of trouble
You, you were a no show

Twanecia Ollivierre

My name is Twanecia Ollivierre. I have a deep love for reading, drawing and writing. Writing for me is the opportunity to be able to express myself freely, to create new worlds and to embrace a new idea with glee.

Crossroads

Help!
My soul screams for rescue
From sadness, pain and hurt
From the consuming rage
Of the pit of hell beneath.

Have mercy!
My soul cries for release
From misery and tears
From turmoil and sin
And from vanity of earthly things.

Forgive Me!
My soul begs for cleansing
From bitterness and hatred
From greed and deceit
From jealousy and envy for things
I can't possess.
Help!

Seduced by Death

Death is omnipresent,
Here, there, everywhere.
Yet he presented himself before me
With a smirk on his porcelain face.
He appeared perfect, harmless.

Hand outstretched,
He compelled me forward with a smile so reassuring,
But behind it, a hidden secret.
He seduced me with his captivating voice.
Taking small steps, I stumbled towards him
Inches away, yet arm's length apart.

Then, his features became clear.
At first, he appeared in the likeness of my lover
His face, one of manly beauty.
But now, I stared at bloated, rotten flesh
That made me hesitant.
I delayed.

Death made promises that seemed irresistible.
He made himself appear easy, since life was hard.
"I am inevitable," he warned me.
"There is no escaping!"
Then he took my hand and dragged me beyond.
I held on to him, and we vanished into the mist.

Epilogue

Timeless

Excuse me.
Do you have the time?
No, no, no. Sorry. Not that time.
The time to answer just one question.
What's the question?
What would you do if you had all the time in the world?
Wait!
Before you answer, just know this:
You don't have all the time in the world.
You can't have all the time in the world.
But you can try.
So, if not all the time, would you settle for more time?
Sounds better?
Ok then, what would you do with more time?
Would you use more time to eat, to drink, and be merry?
More time to sleep?
More time to watch the games?
More time to scroll the timelines,

Read the bad news and good gossip?
More time for PornHub and Only Fans?
More time to smoke and snort?
More time to lie, to steal and to kill?
How much more time would you want?
Surely not all the time in the world,
Because you can't, but you can try.
Time goes by so slowly, and time can do so much.
Time goes by so quickly, and so much is not done.
Don't you wish you could read time?
No. Sorry. Not the magazine.
The seconds. The minutes. The hours.
The days. The weeks. The months.
The years. The decades. The centuries.
The light years.
No. Sorry.
That's distance.
Pay Attention!
The only time you have is now!
Because time has no hands that you can turn back!
Now is the time to call.
Now is the time to text.
Now is the time for the spouse and the babies.
Now is the time to buy that house, the land,
The automobile.
Now is the time for the Bachelors, the Masters, the PHDs.
Now is the time to make the millions,
    the billions, the trillions.
Now is the time to do all the things
    that you would have done
If you had all the time in the world.
But you don't.
Don't even try.
Take your time.

Use the time that you have
To do the things that are timeless.
Take time to love.
Take time to share.
Take time to care.
Take time to plant the seeds,
Trim the stems,
Smell the roses.
Take time to teach.
Take time to learn.
Take time to help.
Take time to trust.
Take time to grow old.
I could go on and on and on
and on and on and on....
But times does not permit.
So maybe another time.
In the meantime;
Thank you for your time.
Hope it was time well spent.

- Junior Jarvis

ACKNOWLEDGMENTS

The authors thank the management and staff at His Majesty's Prison and the Belle Isle Correctional Facility, their mentor Mr. David "Darkie" Williams, Sophia Williams at MindField SVG, Marc Erdrich and Ruth Boerger of Hobo Jungle Press, family members and well-wishers, and all others who contributed to making this dream a reality.

Something out of nothing!